Grandmother's Chair

by Ann Herbert Scott

Illustrated by Meg Kelleher Aubrey

Clarion Books

New York

The full-color artwork in this book
was prepared with watercolors.
The text type is 16 pt. Sabon.

Clarion Books
a Houghton Mifflin Company imprint
215 Park Avenue South, New York, NY 10003
Text copyright © 1990 by Ann Herbert Scott
Illustrations copyright © 1990 by Meg Kelleher Aubrey

Library of Congress Cataloging-in-Publication Data
Scott, Ann Herbert.
Grandmother's chair / by Ann Herbert Scott ; illustrated by Meg
Kelleher Aubrey.
p.   cm.
Summary: Together Grandmother and Katie look through a family
album and find all the little girls who have sat in Katie's black-
and-gold chair.
ISBN 0-395-52001-0
[1. Grandmothers—Fiction.   2. Chairs—Fiction.]   I. Aubrey, Meg
Kelleher, ill.   II. Title.
PZ7.S415Gr   1990
[E]—dc20   89-77725
CIP
AC

WOZ 10 9 8 7 6 5 4 3 2 1

For the little black and gold chair,
all who have sat in it
and all who will sit in it.
— A.H.S.

For my husband Mark
and my son Matthew
— M.K.A.

When Katie came to visit her grandmother, she asked, "Grammy, how did
you ever fit on that little chair?"

"I was little, too," her grandmother
answered. "Just as small as you."

"What did you look like then?"

"Let's see if we can find a picture," said her grandmother, taking down the big leather family album from the bookcase.

Together they sat on the living room couch and turned the pages.

"Look, here's my own mother, your great-grandmother, sitting in the chair when she was a little girl. See her favorite doll and her fancy china tea set? She was a lot like you."

"A lot like me?"

"Yes, a lot like you. She used to tell me how she loved to sing with her mother and listen to her daddy's stories. And at night she watched the stars."

"See if we can find a picture of you," said Katie.

"Look, here I am," said her grand-mother. "It was my fourth birthday, I remember. My mother wrapped the chair in shiny paper and tied it with a big blue bow. I was so excited when I opened the package. The chair was just my size! I put it by the radio where I could sit and listen to the music."

"Were you like me?"

"A lot like you. I sang with my mother and listened to my daddy's stories. And at night I watched the stars."

"Then what happened?"

"At last I grew too big to sit on the chair anymore. We put it up in the attic to keep it safe for another day."

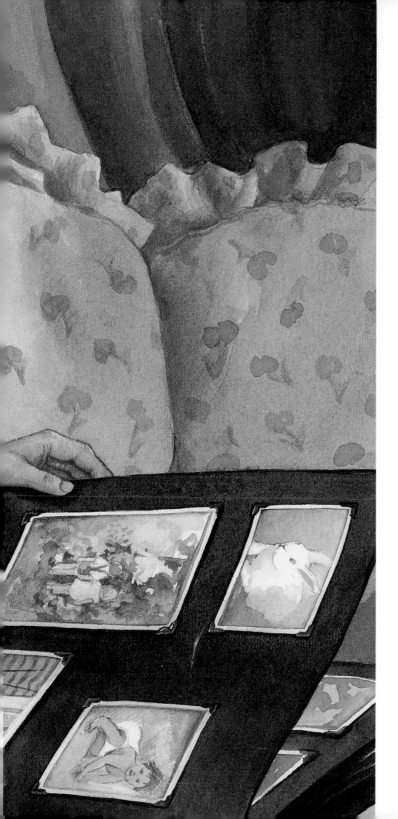

Katie began turning the pages of the album.

"Can you guess who sat on the chair next?" her grandmother asked.

"Mommy," guessed Katie.

"You guessed right. Here she is on *her* fourth birthday. That's the funny green corduroy alligator I made for her. She's sitting by the TV drinking from her favorite red mug with the crazy twisty straw."

"Was she like me?"

"A lot like you. She sang with me and listened to Grandpa's stories. And at night she watched the stars."

"Then what happened?"

"Then it was her turn to grow up. After a while she grew too big to sit on the chair anymore. Up into the attic it went so it would be safe for another day."

"You mean safe for me?" asked
Katie.

"Yes, safe for you to take home
tomorrow. Because now it's your turn
to sing with your mother and listen to
your daddy's stories. And when you
grow up, the little chair will go into
your attic, safe for another day."

"Safe for my own little girl." Katie
smiled as she closed the album.

"I wonder what she'll be like," said her grandmother.

"I know," said Katie. "She'll be a lot like me."

"I wouldn't be surprised," said her grandmother, picking Katie up in her arms.

"But now it's time for bed. Put on
your bathrobe and slippers and let's go
and watch the stars."